A Day With Emily Emeryboard

Written by Ben Smith
Illustrated by Jennifer Cooper

You know, I really hated writing stories at school. Last week I hated our teacher too. We all had to write a story. The teacher said he was going to send our stories to a friend of his who was an author. She would read them and choose the best story.

We had to work on our stories all week. I wrote about a keeper at the zoo. He muddled up all the animals so when the people came to his zoo, they didn't know which animal was which. He muddled up an elephant and a giraffe and a monkey. He ended up with a little elephant with a long neck, swinging in the trees.

I knew my teacher didn't like my story because he kept on at me to change some of the words. The new words were hard to spell so I had to use my dictionary a lot. I did what he said so he would leave me alone.

On Friday he sent our stories to his friend. He told us there would be a prize for the best story. The prize was to spend a whole Saturday with the author.

Yuck! Some prize! A whole day with an author! Her name was Emily Emeryboard. I just knew she would be a wrinkled old prune who talked about nothing but writing stories.

Not that I needed to worry. I knew she would hate reading my story as much as I hated writing it.

How wrong can you be? I won the prize!

All week I thought up clever plans to get out of the day. I even told my teacher I was sick with some very bad disease that killed authors.

I moaned to my parents and begged them to say I couldn't go.

In the end my dad said, "Just go. It's only one day out of your life. You never know, you might even enjoy yourself."

My mother told me to stop fussing. She said she was very proud of me.

So on Saturday morning I got ready for the worst day of my life with Emily Emeryboard.

I was wrong, even though I hate to say it.

Emily Emeryboard came and picked me up at 10 o'clock.

She wasn't old and wrinkled like a prune. In fact she looked like a cross between a peach and a strawberry. She came in a thing that looked like a bathtub on wheels.

"Come on, get in," she said.

I got in and she gave me a helmet to put on.
Then she told me to do up the seatbelt.

"Right," she said as we sped off. "We're going
to the muddled-up-games."

"What are the muddled-up-games?" I asked.

"Wait and see," she replied.

The muddled-up-games were neat fun. There was basketball you played with a tennis ball, and a hockey stick.

Then there was soccer you played with a tennis racket tied to your shoe.

There was even some skateboarding with snowshoes. You could try any game you liked.

Emily Emeryboard and I tried everything and soon it was time to go home.

"Right," she said, before we sped off in her bathtub, "why don't you like writing stories?"

"I can't spell a lot of the words," I said. "And the teacher makes us edit our work and that's boring. I hate it."

"But you have lots of good ideas," she replied. "You have to have good ideas to be an author. You need to edit your stories so your idea is the best it can be. And you have to put the spelling right so other people can read what you've written."

"I suppose so," I said. "Most times I just change the words to the ones I can spell."

"Never, ever, do that again! Do you hear me?" Emily Emeryboard said to me. "Using just easy words spoils your idea and makes your story boring! Good ideas need good words."

We talked about it all the way home. She made me laugh when she told me about some of her best stories and the great words she liked to use.

And guess what? I love writing stories now, and I never, ever, use just the words I can spell. That's way too boring!